YEARBOOK SECTIONS

01 **YEAR**
Record the important details

02 **My Autographs**
Gather the autographs of everyone

03 **Notes and Messages**
Collect important messages from friends, classmates, teachers and family.

04 **My Pic's**
Add photos of your class, friends and family

05 **Contact Details**
Collect contact details to keep in touch!

©**The Life Graduate Publishing Group**

No part of this book may be scanned, reproduced or distributed in any printed or electronic form without the prior permission of the author or publisher.

01

YEAR _____

CLASS _____

Other details

_____
_____
_____

02

My
Autographs

Get everyone to sign their name!

Autographs

Friends, Classmates, Teachers, Family........

Autographs
Friends, Classmates, Teachers, Family........

Autographs

Friends, Classmates, Teachers, Family........

Autographs

Friends, Classmates, Teachers, Family........

Autographs

Friends, Classmates, Teachers, Family........

Autographs

Friends, Classmates, Teachers, Family........

Memories Forever

03
NOTES & MESSAGES

Memories Forever

NOTES & MESSAGES

NOTES & MESSAGES

NOTES & MESSAGES

NOTES & MESSAGES

NOTES & MESSAGES

NOTES & MESSAGES

NOTES & MESSAGES

NOTES & MESSAGES

04

My Pic's

Stick Your Favorite Photos in Here!

PHOTOS

Friends, class photo, graduation pic's........

PHOTOS Friends, class photo, graduation pic's........

PHOTOS  Friends, class photo, graduation pic's........

PHOTOS  Friends, class photo, graduation pic's........

PHOTOS

Friends, class photo, graduation pic's........

PHOTOS Friends, class photo, graduation pic's........

05

Contact Details

Keep in Touch!

CONTACT DETAILS

Name ....

Email ....
Phone ....

Other

Name ....

Email ....

Phone ....

Other

Name ....

Email ....

Phone ....

Other

CONTACT DETAILS

Name ....

Email ....

Phone ....

Other

Name ....

Email ....

Phone ....

Other

Name ....

Email ....

Phone ....

Other

CONTACT DETAILS

Name ....
Email ....
Phone ....

Other

Name ....
Email ....
Phone ....

Other

Name ....
Email ....
Phone ....

Other

CONTACT DETAILS

Name ....

Email ....

Phone ....

Other

Name ....

Email ....

Phone ....

Other

Name ....

Email ....

Phone ....

Other

CONTACT DETAILS

Name ....

Email ....
Phone ....

Other

Name ....

Email ....

Phone ....

Other

Name ....

Email ....

Phone ....

Other

CONTACT DETAILS

Name ....
Email ....
Phone ....

Other

Name ....

Email ....

Phone ....

Other

Name ....

Email ....

Phone ....

Other

CONTACT DETAILS

Name ....

Email ....
Phone ....

Other

Name ....

Email ....

Phone ....

Other

Name ....

Email ....

Phone ....

Other

CONTACT DETAILS

Name ....

Email ....

Phone ....

Other

Name ....

Email ....

Phone ....

Other

Name ....

Email ....

Phone ....

Other

CONTACT DETAILS

Name ....

Email ....

Phone ....

Other

Name ....

Email ....

Phone ....

Other

Name ....

Email ....

Phone ....

Other

CONTACT DETAILS

Name ....

Email ....

Phone ....

Other

Name ....

Email ....

Phone ....

Other

Name ....

Email ....

Phone ....

Other

CONTACT DETAILS

Name ....

Email ....

Phone ....

Other

Name ....

Email ....

Phone ....

Other

Name ....

Email ....

Phone ....

Other

CONTACT DETAILS

Name ....

Email ....
Phone ....

Other

Name ....

Email ....

Phone ....

Other

Name ....

Email ....

Phone ....

Other

CONGRATULATIONS!

www.ingramcontent.com/pod-product-compliance
Lightning Source LLC
LaVergne TN
LVHW081525060526
838200LV00044B/2011